AL

"Acute Ludicrous Leukaemia"

Daigo Fenu

Illustrated by Johan BC

Dear reader,

If you are reading this book right now, you would not want to, this book is full of ridiculousness of neurons and will probably not be suitable for someone like you. I am sorry, but in this body, it's full of ridiculous cells, neurons, weird ways of treatment, for example, a needle near your armpit. I would feel really glad if you would put down this book and hope to find another book by Roald Dahl and probably read this book another time. I would be glad. Hope to find anything good in that book that you have of Roald Dahl, I'm pretty sure. If you have not picked up another book by now, it is best to return this book to the bookshop or library and get another one, if you do not like Roald Dahl.

Thank you,

Daigo Fenu

It's me

Part 1

What is ALL this Diagnosis?

Introduction

Just so you know, I'm 8 years old. I know, I'm a bit young for doing this type of topic but I had an idea of making a story based on my condition T-cell ALL (T-cell acute lymphoblastic leukaemia) and it's quite hilarious! I am the type of guy who makes people laugh, like a comedian, but it doesn't make my mum laugh, haha! This story is about my condition, but in a nicer, better and actually ridiculous way.

Characters throughout this series of books

Who do you think it is, it's me! I'm the main character.

Mum

Dad

Grandma S

Grandma K (Donna)

Grandpa

Luca

Aunt

Neuron 1

Neuron 2

Neuron 3

Neuron 4

Neuron 5

Neuron 6

Doctor Ellie

Doctor Sam

Senior Nurse Sun

Senior Nurse Hallen

Senior Nurse Lour

Nurse Nick (Nicole)

Nurse Ash

Play Specialist Jan

Play Specialist Sara

Miss Minor

Miss Binter

Miss Column

Great-Grandma

Chapter 1
A Starting Point

"What's for the next lesson?" I asked to Miss Minor, on the last school day of the half term.

"Science, Daigo, science." replied Miss Minor.

"Great! For the last day of school before half term, I actually have a science lesson! Oooohh-Ooh-oop!" I exclaimed cheerfully, in a rather funny way.

"Now, don't get carried away, Daigo." said Miss Minor.

"Sorry, miss, am I in trouble?!"

“No, you are not, don’t worry!”

“OK”

A few weeks after, I was going to my play scheme on the 43 bus.

“Ooh, I bagsie the top bunk!” I said cheerfully.

“OK.” my mum said.

Meanwhile, in my body...

‘Daigo’s body has a problem,’ said Neuron 2, ‘and he doesn’t know, what are we gonna do, roll with it?!’

Neuron 2 is sometimes a bit crazy headed, but he warns Neuron 1 everything that is going to happen next, to me!

'I guess,' replied Neuron 1, to this rhetorical question, 'we can't keep it in for a long time, it's a vomit. When it's functioning, we have to make it come out, and before you say it, don't say "from the bottom" because 1,' showing his finger, 'it won't be able to and 2, it is super ridiculous, and don't say "it is possible" or "diarrhoea" because it is the same reason as number two.'

Neuron 1 is intelligent, well, at least, he thinks he is intelligent.

'OK, OK, OK, we will do it, just don't come out in the middle of the operation and say 'actually, we won't do it' unless it's an emergency.'

I vomited, that was their plan, wasn't it? But everybody had to get out in Windsor Terrace bus stop, and I was stopping at Moorfields Eye Hospital, I thought it was a normal hospital so I was thinking 'can we go in that hospital', but now I realised that in the name there was a clue that it wasn't a normal hospital, can you spot it?

I went back home and there was a local GP in front of our house and my mum escorted me there and they checked me up. They thought it was nothing, it would 'go away **soon**'. On another day, I had to go there, and the doctor said again 'It just hasn't gone away, wait a bit longer.' But also my mum had to go there, but I don't know why...

Chapter Two
When Will This (Not Knowing What's Happening) Situation Stop?

Around a week after, I drank some milk and honey and then... I had to go to Italy, I know, I'm sick, but it was already booked... I stopped at the bus stop and then...

I vomited, again...

'Sorry I didn't warn you!' shouted Neuron 3, across the brain.

Neuron 3 is a kind of assistant of Neuron 2, but he doesn't always help Neuron 2, sometimes, he does work on the mouth, what I eat, what I choke and even what I vomit so he is sometimes ridiculous and says 'Daigo has vomited' when Neuron 1 and Neuron 2 already know.

'That's fine!' shouted back Neuron 2, "cos we already know!'

In Italy, I was quite unwell, so I don't remember anything except this...

"Dove stiamo andando?" I asked in Italian, which means 'Where are we going?'.

"Stiamo andando da questo privato dottore, in Olbia." Grandma S replied. Grandma S is 67 years old and is my grandma in Italy and Olbia is a city in Sardinia, Italy and this sentence means we are going to this private doctor, in Olbia.

The road was a bit like it had still been under construction and the paint was going away but the doctor's house was on a road near the tranquil Tyrrhenian Sea in the Mediterranean. It was almost 30 degrees Celsius but it's normal for Sardinia. I even remember my auntie's wedding day, which was 37 degrees Celsius in Sardinia, I had to wear three layers, **three**.

This doctor was so quiet, I couldn't hear a word he was saying. I think I had a problem with my ears at that time, but even my dad couldn't hear him, so that kind of proves he's quiet.

"Apri l tua bocca," he whispered, which means 'Open your mouth,' in Italian. He repeated the same phrase again and again until I finally heard him properly and opened my mouth. The doctor gave my dad some type of liquid for my nose (I thought it was for my ears) and then we went back to my grandma's (auntie's) house in Porto San Paolo.

Porto San Paolo is a kind of municipality in Sardinia and, if you go to the sea, you can see the beautiful and independent Isola di Tavolara, which means Tavolara Island. Everywhere you go in Porto San Paolo, you can see this long and wide island.

Grandma S

Grandma S' (or my auntie's) house is a house made of rock and has a big garden where she has figs and cactuses, she also has two entrances of her house and only one has a post-box.

While I was coming back from Sardinia, I always wanted to lie down, on the train and on the plane.

I saw a picture of myself about a year later and, boy, I looked green. I looked as green as a very light green leaf.

When I came back home, in England, I went to another doctor when I tried to go to school and, this doctor said, 'It's just an infection, that's all!' and I was like 'Fine(!)'.

An hour later, I said to my mum "When will this (not knowing what's happening) situation stop?"

My mum started to cry, "I don't know, I really don't know."

A few days later, I finally saw a doctor in the GP in front of my house telling me to go to Whittington Hospital, Archway, London, and a nurse did a blood test on me, a cannula test, to be precise.

Neuron 4 appeared in the brain, 'We're having a blood test done in a cannula!'

Neuron 4 warns everything from the fingers to the shoulders, he's the hand warning man!

Neuron 1 was shocked, 'Really, I don't know, the nurse said to face this way to the wall that has many famous London landmarks, which is quite nice. Wait, hold on, what is a cannula?'

'A cannula' replied Neuron 4, 'is a needle that goes into your hand and takes blood out to do blood tests.'

'Ooooohhhh,' said Neuron 1, 'well, this is a nurse, she has trained for years to do this job, hospitals would never put us into danger letting some random trainee doctor to do this blood test on Daigo!'...

Chapter 3

'I Hate You!!!'

At one point of the day, I went to a room in Whittington Hospital and I saw a trainee doctor and I was like 'Hi', but Neuron 1 forgot to send the message in my brain...

'Are you seriously serious?' shouted Neuron 1. 'What I thought wouldn't happen happened. What I said wasn't a wish!'

'Don't send it!' said Neuron 2. 'It'll only make Daigo worse!'

'How?' said Neuron 1, quite casually.

'Because it'll only make Daigo worry and he'll say 'I'm getting out of this room''

Well, that was kind of what I said, the doctor was putting a blood test needle inside the bone on your arm that goes towards your arm and the bone that goes to the shoulder.

"I hate you!!!" I yelled. My dad was in the same room, so I said it to him when he was holding my hand.

Finally, she gave up after a few minutes, if you've seen the bruise on my arm, it was stood there for about 6 months, I had to kind of peel it off when the bruised skin was dry and popping out.

Neuron 1

I went to my ward and one time, on the same day, the nurse was taking care of me, I had a bandage around my cannula, and they had to unwrap the bandage to put a new one and the bandage roll just went rolling on the floor! And I saw a Spider-Man sticker on top of the cannula!

6 hours after that, which the time after 6 hours was about 2:30am, they had to bring me to a hospital, if you have been transported to a different hospital from Whittington Hospital, then you might know where I was going, if not...

Chapter 4

Where is Great Ormond Street Hospital?

Sorry about the last chapter, I seriously can't tell you until later on. I can only give you hints that it is a real, big hospital and it is for children. It's the best hospital that I've ever went to and staff are the best.

"I'm so tired," I told my dad. "what's the time?"

"The time is a couple of minutes past 2:00am." My dad replied, looking at a digital clock in the ambulance, which was wrong-as the time was 2:30.

My dad

We had arrived at about 2:45am and I saw a random colour sofa, and, on my ward, I slept, I just didn't care what was the time or the place that I was at, I just slept with my dad sleeping on a lower-built bed on my right, but one thing I thought is, **what is going on?**

The next day, when I started to completely wake up on my automatic bed, I said to my dad, "Where are we?"

"We are in GOSH."

"What do you mean by GOSH, you mean by the saying gosh or..."

"No, GOSH is a short way of saying Great Ormond Street Hospital."

"Alright, but where is Great Ormond Street Hospital?"

"GOSH is a famous hospital..." my dad replied.

"What's it famous for?"

"It's famous for its most famous charity campaign, I forgot what it was called, but the main thing is Peter Pan book owners around the world pay and the amount they pay go to this hospital, Great Ormond Street Hospital for Children."

"For children?"

"Yes."

"OK, what were you saying before?"

"Oh, right, GOSH is a famous hospital..."

"You already said that,"

"Let me finish, GOSH is a famous hospital and is located in the area close to Russell Square Station."

"OK, but the first bit you already said."

"Does it really matter?"

In my brain...

'Should we shrug?' said Neuron 2.

'OK, yeah!' replied Neuron 1.

I shrugged. Silently.

'Just one thing, don't type it in the thingy*, but come to the spleen with me, I need to show you something that's happening.'

'OK.' replied Neuron 2.

They slid down to the spleen through the veins...

'W H A T O N E A R T H?' exclaimed Neuron 2, talking word by word.

'Yup, there are many white blood cells than you think.' Said Neuron 1.

"But they're so tiny, what has this pandemonium got to do with staying in a hospital, and it probably feels like we will be here for nearly a year."

Actually, reader, I know, it's like the normal, grown white blood cells have just had babies and the babies are multiplying and the babies are not controllable which means it doesn't know what to do and then they are named in the cartoonish way, 'bad cells' but in the scientific way, it's called 'leukaemia cells' or 'lymphocytes'.

Outside the body, Doctor Sam came in my room and said "Hi, I'm Doctor Sam' and let my mum (she's here!) and dad read a document about my condition and then after, he examined me and then after an hour he entered, he went.

Half an hour later, an anaesthetist and a surgeon came in my cubicle and she said I'm having a surgery done in a few hours and let my dad sign a letter for my surgery to accept what is happening today and they told me that they are going to put a port in, I had no idea what it was.

Doctor Sam

Then Nurse Ash came into the room and demonstrated what is going to happen by a dummy body...

"So, this yellow circle is called the port and then," she said, opening the part next to the breast, "they'll tighten it up in here."

After a while my surgery started, although Neuron 1 and Neuron 2 were at the same place where they were doing the surgery.

'Aaaaaaaaahhhhhhh, what is going on here, it looks like they completely opened the place next to the breast, whatever it's called, does it really have a name?' questioned Neuron 1.

'Hold on, I put Daigo on auto-memory, maybe somebody told him something about this big black hole.' shouted Neuron 2, remembering what he did.

They rushed to the brain to check what is going on...

'OK, so, chat chat chat, aha, got it, it says that an anaesthetist and a surgeon came, and the anaesthetist told Daigo 'We're having a surgery done next to the breast.' And then a nurse came to demonstrate what's going to be done.'

The next day was a special day, it was Father's Day! So the kitchen were selling brownies for the fathers' coffees but my dad wasn't here at the time when they were selling brownies so I just ate one, but then, after that, a shocking present arrived from my dad's friend, it was a LEGO construction toy, so I ate and then I went on playing the LEGO, then, another doctor, came into my room and she seemed very jolly, wasn't a very jolly moment, at first I was all smiley and then she had a needle that had something that looked like yellow wings on the other end of the needle. Before, I had anaesthetic cream on where they had the port put in, she told me to take it off, wait, hold on, what, a needle?

*A thingy in this sentence is a kind of computer or sending device that sends sentences or words to let me speak

Chapter 5

Why Has It Got Yellow Wings On?

"What's that?" I asked the doctor.

"This?" asked the doctor.

"Yes!" I said to the doctor, straight after she said the word.

"This is a port needle; you know where you can see those stitches?"

"Oh, they're stitches," I exclaimed, "I watch Operation Ouch! and I never knew stitches looked like this because they look really different, but yes, I can see them stitches."

"And I am going to put this needle just below it, it might hurt but just don't freak ou..."

"What? Please don't do it! It's really scary!"

"...t. It's fine, it's fine!" she said, but at the same time trying to put the needle in the port.

My dad was on the bed next to me and he helped me, "Aaaaahhhhh, I hate you!!!!!!!!!!!" and I can't believe I said that again!

A port can actually take blood out from the body because of how near it is to the veins.

The doctor finally put it in...or did she? She tried to take the blood out from the port...nothing came! And what a nightmare it was afterwards! Because she couldn't take out the blood from the port, she had to reposition it, which meant that she had to take out the port needle and try and get it in the right place!!! Wow! How scared I was, you would imagine before and now! Wow! And I said it again, was I supposed to, does it say on the script, I'm having it next to me! And also another exclamation mark, great(!) And another one! And another one! And another one, I could go on and on, but I won't, let's get on with the story! And another one...

I asked the doctor after crying, "Why has it got yellow wings on?" but she just replied, "It just does, it might help with the tissue below it but apart from that, nothing, really, but it looks weird to me."

So what happens next, you're thinking, well, basically nothing but I could tell you all the fun bits that happened to me until the next chapter, because it says here that one chapter has to be minimum 2 pages long so let's get on! And another one! And...

So because I wasn't at school, I had to have a school, luckily, GOSH (Great Ormond Street Hospital) has a hospital school and quite a good one! And another one. And that meant I had to go to school, not go to, how would I, with a port needle stuck to a pole, no, no, no, the teacher would come to the cubicle and we would do fun things such as:

- Make slime
- Make things explode
- Word searches
- Projects on animals
- Projects on what I like
- Making gloves nearly explode, which meant to make big hands

and more...

You would think that's all, but it's not, you would never know what you would do until you find out or when it's too late and then you find out or see that it might be fun things or boring things, but you never know! And another one. And you can see friends coming to give you presents or you get a prize for bravery! And another one...

But this is all of the fun bits, after all that, I have to take the medication and every day it's hard, because I take tablets, it might or might not be an easy thing to do and you might have not had a tablet, I never did and I'm starting to take them now. So every day I have to take 3-5 tablets in the night and sometimes 2 in the morning. So I have quite a struggle taking them.

"What is this?" I asked to the nurse.

"These are tablets." replied the nurse.

"Oh, I heard of them in school, I thought they meant tablets as in digital tablets!"

"No, these are tablets!"

"OK, so do I put them in my mouth, does it dissolve?" I asked when I never wanted to use the word dissolve.

"No," said the nurse, "you have to swallow it with water."

I gulped, "Should I worry if I choke or not?"

"No." the nurse said, thinking how many times she had to say the word 'no'.

"OK. Bye."

"Bye."

Inside my mouth...

'So,' Neuron 3 thought, 'if she said all that, then that means there is nothing to worry about, but I still have to tell Neuron 2, but I also have to stay in the mouth.

He had to choose between going to the brain to warn Neuron 2 or staying in the mouth.

'I'll go to the brain,' said Neuron 3.

In the brain...

'So she said about the tablets, Neuron 3 will take care of it!' said Neuron 1.

'So the nurse said about taking tablets and said that there's nothing to worry about, so I guess there's nothing to worry about, right?' panted Neuron 3.

The place was silent.

'You are really stupid, Mr, not really Mr, maybe, Sir, or mate, or Neuron, Neuron is better, anywhoo, you just left the department that Daigo is going to swallow the tablets.' said Neuron 2.

'But you needed to know, I rushed here to tell you!' shouted Neuron 3 and was really surprised that he could shout so loud out of breath.

'We knew, we work in the brain, we know you work in the mouth and can still hear but we know too because we work in the department that is about speaking, we order the mouth, not you, the mouth, to speak and we can hear every single move and speech that everybody does close to us!!! And now Daigo is going to choke because YOU LEFT YOUR DEPARTMENT, THE DEPARTMENT THAT THE TABLETS ARE SUPPOSED TO GO IN!!!!!!!!!' shouted Neuron 1.

'OK, OK, I'll go back!' said Neuron 3.

'Don't, by the time you go back, he would choke because he WASN'T CONTROLLED BY YOU!'

'Please, we just have to let him choke!' said Neuron 2.

Outside the brain, in the actual world...

I choked, a lot...

"Cough! Cough! Cough!, Cough! Cough!, Cough!, Cough! Cough!" I choked and then I drank water, I felt better.

In the brain...

'And now you have to go, now!!!' shouted Neuron 1.

And it was easier after a couple more times, but it was never very easy or very, very easy. And I hoped the next day was fun, and it was...

Chapter 6
Colourful Beads

So the next day, Nurse Ash came into the room and was showing me these beads. I did not have a clue what it was for, but Nurse Ash explained to me.

"Can you look at these beads?"

"For what?"

"Well, you don't have to, but these beads are for courage and by the end of your treatment, you will have tonnes. Here is a list of collectable beads. The ones I ticked means you got one of them, the ones I numbered are the ones that you got more than one."

She lent me the book, "Bone Marrow Aspirate | Biopsy | Aspirations | Joint Injections | EVD : Beige... Visits from Care Team (Occupational Therapy | Respiratory Therapy | Physiotherapy) : Rainbow... Long Term Follow-Up & Comprehensive Visit : Glass Selection. Alright, I won't have a chance to get all of those in this period!"

"You know what you will be getting the most?"

"Which one?"

"These," she pointed at the book, "White, Blue and Light Purple, for sure you will get a community visit, which is light purple!"

"What's a community visit?"

Nurse Ash

"A community visit is a nurse coming to your home to take a blood test."

"How?"

"She or he brings all the equipment and they keep the equipment in your house."

"OK, what is steroid? It says that blue is steroid!"

"Steroid is a type of medicine that can cure many diseases, but some make you want to be hungry or to eat a particular food regularly."

"Alright."

In my body...

'Thanks for that message, Neuron 1!' Neuron 5 said.

Neuron 5 is a calm neuron that works for the stomach (apparently!).

'So, what can I force the workers down in the stomach to remind themselves, because we already took the steroid once?' he thought.

'OK, so maybe I can warn them when the next tablet is going to come, or they can deal it with themselves? I know, I'll tell them, watch out for lots of food coming down from the oesophagus! Great idea! Actually, I could've thought about that earlier.'

So he did tell them to watch out, but the workers clearly did not know what a lot meant, so they were just calm...

Outside the body...

“Hom, Hom, Hom!” I ate.

Back inside the body...

‘AAAAAAAHHHHHHHHHHH!!!!!!!!!!!’ the first worker yelled.

‘What’s this?’ shouted the second worker.

‘Tonnes of food, I guess.’ replied the third worker.

‘What on earth did I tell you, there were lots of food coming your way!!!’ shouted Neuron 5.

'Sorry!" said all of the workers at once.

Outside my body...

"I'm stuffed!" I exclaimed.

"You know why, you just ate 5 portions of Japanese sushi, that's why!" said my dad.

"Alright, I remember mum telling me about somebody coming tomorrow, do you have any idea of who it is?" I asked my dad.

"Nope(!)" replied my dad sarcastically.

"OK?" I said.

Chapter 7
My Teacher?

"Wait, hold on, my teacher, you mean, Miss Minor?" I asked my dad.

"Yes, and the next-door teacher, too." replied my dad.

"OK, when, what time?"

"Around 6:00pm because they have to finish marking children's books and go to meetings, probably."

"OK! I'm really excited!"

"But, after that you still have to take the..."

I closed my eyes and spoke, **"DO NOT SPOIL IT FOR ME."**

"OK."

In my body, they are also getting very excited about Miss Minor coming...

'Yay!' Neuron 1 jumped up and down.

Everyone else jumped up and down too.

At six o'clock in the afternoon...

"Where's Miss Minor?" I asked my mum and dad.

"Give them some time!" my mum said.

Outside the door of the ward, Miss Minor and the other teacher are blocked because they cannot pass through the door...

"Let's try our passes(!)" Miss Minor said.

"It did not work." said the other teacher.

"Of course it didn't, it was sarcasm. You should know if you studied to be a teacher in university."

The door opened.

"It opened? How?"

"What?"

"You leant on the right button!" exclaimed Miss Minor.

"OK, now which cubicle was it, definitely not this one, there's a baby in here, Daigo is not a baby, and this one has a baby too, here we are. Hi!" she waved.

"Hi, Miss!" I said.

"Hi, Daigo. How are you?"

"Good!"

"I'm good too, I have not seen you for a long time!"

"Me neither."

"I also have a few things for you."

"OK."

The other teacher took out an album of pictures, "So this a 'get well soon' album from everyone in your class."

"Wow, is this everyone?"

"Yes, approximately, and also me and the assistant teacher."

"That's a lot of little booklets!"

"And I also got some books from the school library to **keep**!"

"Keep? Don't you have to return them?"

"Yes, but I asked the headteacher to give you special permission to keep these books forever."

"Great!"

We talked and talked until it was time to take my medicine and how horrible it was again.

"Cough! Cough! Cough!, Cough! Cough!, Cough!, Cough! Cough!" I choked and coughed.

Then after that, not actually after that, it took me actually three hours to take because of how scared I was, but after that, I had a good night's sleep and tomorrow was a couple of days before my dismissal in the hospital, yay, I think...

Chapter 8
Goodbye and a Bell

So, today was the day before the dismissal day and it was nice and sunny outside. I actually started to say goodbye to some people because they work in night shifts, but the rest was a wait till tomorrow.

"I don't want to leave, this is the best place because of all these nice people." I said to my mum.

"I know but your time in hospital has finished, for other people it's not. Other people want to finish their treatment so we should let other people use this cubicle. And also, don't worry, this is not the last time we will be in GOSH."

"Wait, it's not the last time?"

"No, you will still need to come here for medicines that do not go in your mouth."

"Can you shorten that sentence?"

My mum sighed, "No you will still need to come here for intrathecal chemotherapy."

"Long words, anyway, did you see a bell in the corridor?"

"Yes?"

"Do you know what that is for?" I asked.

"No, shall we ask the nurse when she comes to do observations?"

"Yeah, good idea!"

Two hours later, Nurse Ash came into the room...

"Hi!" said Nurse Ash.

"Hi, you know that bell in the corridor?"

"Yes?"

"What's it for?"

"Oh, the bell is for when you finish your treatment, but that means not when you get out of hospital, it is when you finish taking medicines and intrathecal chemotherapies."

My mum

"Oh, how long is my treatment, roughly?"

"OK, let me see, intensive care is 2 months, maintenance is two years, this period is six months, around 2020 summer holidays, seeing as this year is 2017."

"Three years?! I mean, three years?"

"Yes, well, no, I would say you would struggle with your chemotherapy for one year, because the rest of the two years are literally nothing, you can live a normal life, except for having raw fish, uncooked meat, maybe not reheated foods, definitely not kept-warm foods and no double-reheated foods."

"So, raw fish?"

“Yes.”

“Uncooked meat?”

“Yes.”

“Reheated foods...”

“Kept-warm foods and double reheated foods, done, and that means in 2020, you will ring this bell and say, ‘my treatment is done, and I am on my way’.”

“To where?”

“Nowhere, actually, somewhere, you can go to your dream place after your treatment...”

“LEGOLAND...” I said.

“Yeah, literally anywhere, even the LEGOLAND in Denmark!”

"Really?"

"But, you don't have to decide now, you do still have three years!"

"Alright!"

She did my observations, if you do not know what observations are in medical treatment like my treatment, observations are a short way of saying pulse, checking your breath and your temperature.

"Thanks for the explanation!" I spoke when she was starting to leave the cubicle.

"You're welcome!"

In my brain...

'I would love to go to LEGOLAND in Denmark!' Neuron 1 whispered.

'Well, we will have to wait for three years in 2020 to go there. Anyways, tomorrow is dismissal day, we will miss everybody, so we will have to say goodbye to everybody tomorrow!' said Neuron 2 excitedly.

'I know, I'm not dumb!' shouted Neuron 1.

'But, apparently, we need Doctor Sam's permission to leave, so when he comes in tomorrow, that will probably be the time we are able to leave.'

'Alright, so Doctor Sam has to come in, right!'

Outside the body, it was already the night...

"Well, tomorrow is dismissal day and at the start of the day, we have to already start packing up, but first, you have to get de-accessed, as they say in hospital!" my mum spoke happily.

De-accessed means when you take out the port needle from the port if you are having a blood test in there or taking chemotherapy in there, for whatever reason you have.

"So there are many things going on tomorrow, we also have to say bye to play specialist Jay!" I said.

"Yeah, that is a good idea too! Well, good night, see you tomorrow on dismissal day!"

"Alright, good night."

"Good night."

This day was quite a dark day, surprisingly, and also, mum started to get so worn out, but why?

Chapter 9

Dismissed

"Today's dismissal day! Yay!" I was really excited today, but first, Nurse Nick, or Nicole, came in to take my port needle out.

"Hi. My name is Nicole. I heard you are scared of these port needles, but do not worry, the only part that will hurt is the 'peeling off the dressing' part, which is peeling off the transparent sticker that you can see there. The rest is taking out the port needle which will, I am one hundred percent sure that will not hurt."

Nurse Nicole

"OK." I said nervously.

"Don't worry," my mum started to speak, "I've had a blood test before and the taking out part does not hurt at all."

"OK." I repeated.

Nicole took out the needle and she was right, it did not hurt at all, there was just some blood coming out of the port, but she said it's normal because that is the veins that the needle was put in, and then she gave me a plaster for the bleeding.

"Bye, I'll see you soon!" said Nicole sadly.

"Bye." me and my mum said at the same time.

My mum suddenly spoke, “Well, let’s start packing up.”

“Yeah, good idea, now that I am not stuck to a pole.”

We started packing up books, DVDs, toys, digital stuff, clothes, everything. Then Doctor Sam came into the room.

“Hi, Doctor Sam.” I exclaimed.

“Hi, now, mum, Daigo is able to go, if he needs to do anything before he goes, that is not a problem, our next patient is going to come around four o’clock in the afternoon, seeing as the time now is, um,” looking at his watch, “twenty past 12, you can go anytime.”

“Thanks, doc.” I said.

"You're welcome, bye, we will see you soon, I'm sure."

"OK, bye."

"Well, that was early timing," my mum said, "let's wait until dad comes and we also have to wait for the taxi cab so, we will have to wait."

Just a few seconds after, dad came into the room.

"Hi, dad." I said.

"Hi, just so you know, the taxi is already here, so, do you want to say bye to everybody with mum and I will bring everything down to the taxi."

"Yeah, good idea." I said.

"OK, say bye to everybody."

I came out of the cubicle and said bye to everybody, even the play specialist.

I went downstairs, and I also heard from aunt, who came in a few days ago, that Grandma S is going to come to London, so that's exciting. I went downstairs, said goodbye to the hospital, and went back home in Holloway.

Special Thanks to:

GOSH for treating and taking care of me, especially Elephant and Safari Ward.

Whittington Hospital's Ifor Ward, Clinic 4D and the lab for checking on me whenever I felt sick.

Johan for brilliant and flawless manga illustrations.

Nancy for editing with a critical eye

Mum and Dad for helping me publish this book

My brother for jumping while I wrote this book

My grandpa in Japan for, without me asking, translated this book all in Japanese.

And finally, everyone else who supported me along the way

L - #0219 - 040920 - C0 - 216/140/4 - PB - DID2901031